THE Hokey Pokey

PICTURES BY

Sheila Hamanaka

WORDS BY

Larry La Prise, Charles P. Macak, AND Taftt Baker

Simon & Schuster Books for Young Readers

To my niece,
Valentine Marquesa—
welcome to the world

—S. H.

Words and Music by
LARRY LA PRISE
CHARLES P. MACAK
TAFT BAKER

The Hokey Pokey

SIMON & SCHUSTER BOOKS FOR YOUNG READERS
An imprint of Simon & Schuster Children's Publishing Division
1230 Avenue of the Americas, New York, New York 10020
The Hokey Pokey written by Charles P. Macak, Taftt Baker and Larry La Prise
© Copyright 1950, Renewed 1978 Acuff-Rose Music, Inc.
International Rights Secured.
All Rights Reserved.
Used by Permission.
Illustrations copyright © 1997 by Sheila Hamanaka. All rights reserved including the right of reproduction in
whole or in part in any form. SIMON & SCHUSTER BOOKS FOR YOUNG READERS is a trademark of Simon & Schuster.
Book design by Paul Zakris. The text of this book is set in 30-point Pike. The illustrations are rendered in acrylic.
Manufactured in the United States of America. First Edition 10 9 8 7 6 5 4 3 2 1
LIBRARY OF CONGRESS CATALOGING-IN-PUBLICATION DATA
La Prise, Larry.
The hokey pokey / words by Larry La Prise, Charles P. Macak, and Taftt Baker : pictures by Sheila Hamanaka.
p.   cm.
Summary: A lively group of people and animals dances to the lyrics and music of this popular novelty tune.
ISBN 0-689-80519-5
1. Children's songs—Texts.   [1. Dancing—Songs and music.   2. Songs.]   I. Macak, Charles P.
II. Baker, Taftt.   III. Hamanaka, Sheila, ill.   IV. Title.
PZ8.3.L112Ho 1997   782.42164'0268—dc20   [E] 95-43533
CIP AC

The author and publisher gratefully acknowledge the Opryland Music Group, Inc.,
for information on the background of "The Hokey Pokey."

You put your Right Foot in

You put your right foot out

You put your right foot in

And you shake it all about

You do The Hokey Pokey

And you turn yourself around

That's what it's all about.

You put your Left Foot in

You put your left foot out

You put your left foot in

And you shake it all about

You do The Hokey Pokey

And you turn yourself around

That's what it's all about.

You put your Right Arm in

You put your right arm out

You put your right arm in

And you shake it all about

You do The Hokey Pokey

And you turn yourself around

That's what it's all about.

You put your Left Arm in

You put your left arm out

You put your left arm in

And you shake it all about

You do The Hokey Pokey

And you turn yourself around

That's what it's all about.

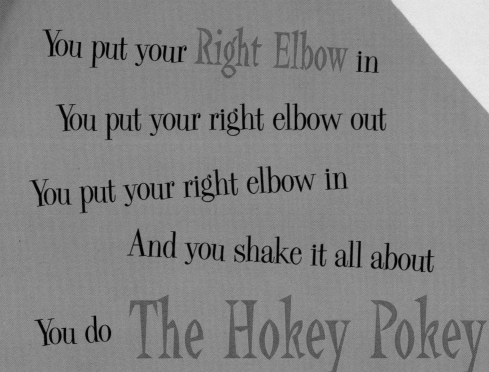

You put your Right Elbow in

You put your right elbow out

You put your right elbow in

And you shake it all about

You do The Hokey Pokey

And you turn yourself around

That's what it's all about.

You put your Left Elbow in

You put your left elbow out

You put your left elbow in

And you shake it all about

You do The Hokey Pokey

And you turn yourself around

That's what it's all about.

You put your **Head** in

You put your head out

You put your head in

And you shake it all about

You do

The Hokey Pokey

And you turn yourself around

That's what it's all about.

You put your **Right Hip** in

You put your right hip out

You put your right hip in

And you shake it all about

You do **The Hokey Pokey**

And you turn yourself around

That's what it's all about.

You put your Left Hip in

You put your left hip out

You put your left hip in

And you shake it all about

You do

The Hokey Pokey

And you turn yourself around

That's what it's all about.

You put your Whole Self in
You put your whole self out
You put your whole self in
And you shake it all about
You do The Hokey Pokey
And you turn yourself around
That's what it's all about.

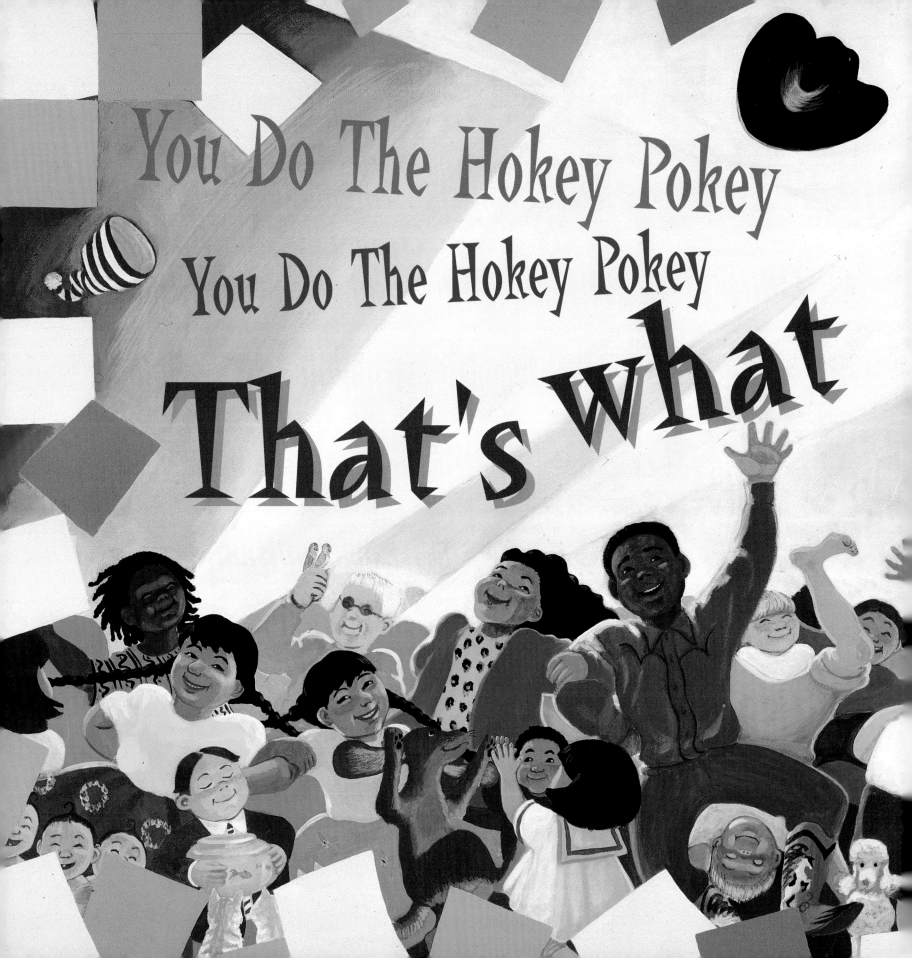

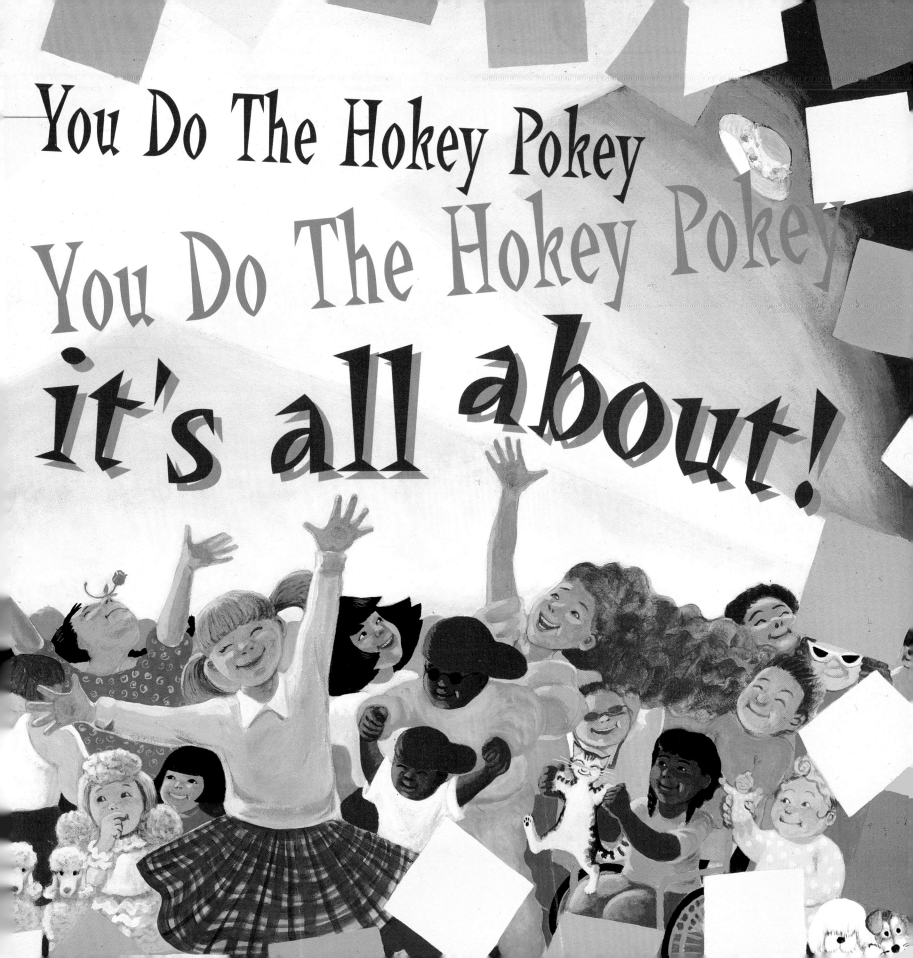

About "The Hokey Pokey"

People first began to sing and dance "The Hokey Pokey" in the late 1940s at the Sun Valley Inn, a glamorous ski resort in Sun Valley, Idaho, that attracted vacationers from all over the country. Larry La Prise, Charles Mason, and Taftt Baker, who played together at the inn as the Sun Valley Trio, decided that the guests needed a fun, easy-to-learn dance everyone could do together. The idea for the song came from an old French song that Larry La Prise's father used to sing and added movements from the square dance and the Lambeth Walk, another popular dance of the time. The new dance caught on so well as an icebreaker that the Sun Valley Trio made a recording, which was released nationwide by the 4 Star Record Company. At campuses, parties, and dance halls, "The Hokey Pokey" was a hit. And people have been putting their right feet in and their left feet out ever since!